GALLOP OFF AND GO!

Diane Wilmer

Illustrated by Valeria Petrone

GALLERY BOOKS
An Imprint of W. H. Smith Publishers Inc.
112 Madison Avenue
New York City 10016

Charlotte was a
very spoiled girl.

"I want a computer," she said to her dad,

and she got one.

"I want a bike," she said to her mom, and she got one.

"I want a radio," she said to her grandmother,

and she got one.

But when she went to Miss Gallopoff's Riding School, Charlotte didn't get what she wanted.

"I want to ride *that* pony!" she said.
"No!" said Miss Gallopoff.
"You can't ride that one yet. That's Rocket. You must ride the other ponies to start with."

So Charlotte did.
Lord Lee was too fast,

Hot Chocolate was frisky.

Sausage was silly,

and Pickle was risky.

Flap-Jack was foolish,

and Bluebell was lazy.

Sunny was slow,

and Daisy was crazy!

"I want to ride Rocket!" said Charlotte again.
"Not yet," said Miss Gallopoff.
"Why not?" asked Charlotte.
"You must learn to ride on the other ponies first,"
said Miss Gallopoff.

How stupid! thought Charlotte.

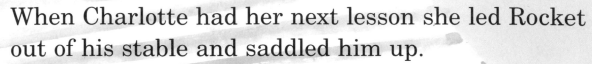

When Charlotte had her next lesson she led Rocket
out of his stable and saddled him up.
Then she climbed onto
his back and flicked the reins.
"Giddyup!" she yelled.
Rocket didn't move.

"Go!" she shouted.
But Rocket wasn't going anywhere.

Charlotte whacked his bottom.
"MOVE YOU LAZYBONES!" she roared.
Rocket shook his head.

"Silly girl," shouted Miss Gallopoff.
"Rocket doesn't like beginners."

"He's going to like *me!*" cried Charlotte.
And she gave poor Rocket a kick in the ribs.
WHACK!

Rocket snorted, kicked up his back legs and sent
Charlotte flying into a mud puddle.
SPLAT!

"I told you so," said Miss Gallopoff.

The other riders laughed and pointed at Charlotte.
"Smarty pants!"
"Know-it-all!"
"Show off!"
"Ugh! Smelly!" they yelled.
Charlotte was very angry.
I'll show you all! she thought.

Every lesson after that she rode one of the
other ponies.
Sam, Hot Chocolate, Sausage and Pickle.
Flap-Jack, Bluebell, Daisy and even Lord Lee.

She learned to mount,

sit,

walk

and trot—

gallop,

canter,

jump

and stop.

"Good," said Miss Gallopoff.
"Very, very good."
Charlotte enjoyed herself so much that

she forgot how angry she'd been with the other riders and made friends with them instead.

She even forgot about Rocket. But Miss Gallopoff had not forgotten.

"Charlotte, I'd like you to ride Rocket in the show jumping competition," said Miss Gallopoff one day.

"No, thank you," said Charlotte.
"Why not?" asked Miss Gallopoff.
"Rocket doesn't like beginners," said Charlotte.
"I'll ride one of the other ponies instead."
"No, you won't," said Miss Gallopoff. "You're
not a beginner anymore."

The day of the competition came.
Charlotte led Rocket out of his stable. She was
very, very nervous.
First she stroked him and tickled his ears, then she
climbed up, nice and slow.

"Good boy," she said. "Good boy."
She squeezed her knees gently into his sides and flicked the reins.
"Giddyup," she said softly—and Rocket moved.

Clip-Clop. Clip-Clop. Straight into the ring.
The jumps were very high and they were close
together, too.

Oh, help! thought Charlotte.
But Rocket loved it. He tossed his head and
neighed. He couldn't wait to get started.

"Number 3!" boomed Miss Gallopoff.
"Charlotte Manners on Rocket."
Charlotte and Rocket trotted towards the first jump.
"Go for it, boy!" squeaked Charlotte—and
Rocket went.

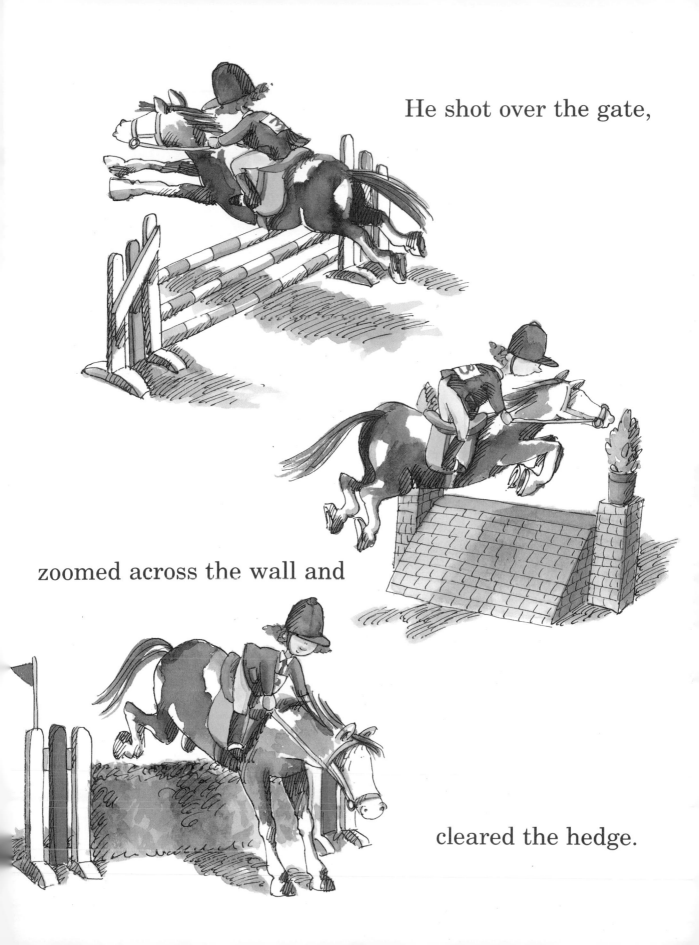

He shot over the gate,

zoomed across the wall and

cleared the hedge.

Then he headed for the corner, flew over the water jump,

zipped across the bar

and finished in record time.
"Hurray! Hurray!" cheered the crowd.
"Well done, you two," said Miss Gallopoff.

Charlotte hugged Rocket, and kissed him.
"You're brilliant," she whispered. "The best
little pony in the world."
Rocket stamped his feet and neighed loudly.
This new girl wasn't so bad after all!